...too far from home

...too far from home

Naomi Shmuel
Illustrated by Avi Katz

First American edition published in 2020 by Kar-Ben Publishing

First published as *Rainbow Child* in 2000 by Hakibbutz Hameyuchad/Sifriyat Poalim Publishing
Published by arrangement with Hakibbutz Hameyuchad/Sifriyat Poalim Publishing

KAR-BEN PUBLISHING®
An imprint of Lerner Publishing Group, Inc.
241 First Avenue North
Minneapolis, MN 55401 USA

Website address: www.karben.com

Additional image: hudiemm/Getty Images (paper).

Main body text set in Bembo Std regular.
Typeface provided by Monotype Typography.

Library of Congress Cataloging-in-Publication Data

Names: Shmuel, Naomi, author. | Katz, Avi, illustrator.
Title: Too far from home / Naomi Shmuel ; illustrated by Avi Katz.
Description: Minneapolis, MN : Kar-Ben Publishing, [2020] | Series: Kar-Ben for older readers | Summary: Eleven-year-old Meskerem, half-Ethiopian and half-American, faces prejudice when she enters a new school just as Israel is coping with a large influx of new immigrants from Ethiopia.
Identifiers: LCCN 2019007627| ISBN 9781541546714 (th : alk. paper)
Subjects: | CYAC: Moving, Household—Fiction. | Prejudices—Fiction. | Schools—Fiction. | Ethiopians—Israel—Fiction. | Jews—Israel—Fiction. | Israel—Fiction.
Classification: LCC PZ7.1.S5142 Cal 2020 | DDC [Fic]—dc23

LC record available at https://lccn.loc.gov/2019007627

Manufactured in the United States of America
1-45649-41662-8/20/2019

To my multicultural children Daniel Achenefe,
Michael Fassil, Yigal Tadele, and Eyal Sunbetu
—N.S.

Chapter 1
Leaving

I looked out my window, trying to soak up the view. If I craned my neck, I could just about see the grassy tip of Mount Hermon, where my sisters and I go sledding every winter. I just couldn't believe that tomorrow I would be waking up in a completely new bedroom. In an apartment building. In the city. With a view that I could not even begin to imagine. So, on that morning, when everybody else got up as usual, I stayed in bed.

"Meskerem, get up! You know what a big day it is today!" My mother's anxious voice reached me from the living room, or what was left of it. The house was already almost empty. All of our belongings were neatly packed away in dozens of cardboard boxes lining the walls and piled up in the hallway. Even my room looked unfriendly. The bare white walls looked so shabby without all my cute animal posters.

I knew that other people were coming to live in our house, people I would never meet. Another kid would sleep in my room, and I would be far away, living a different life a long way from all of my friends.

"Macy, you need to get up, sweetie." My dad gently patted my shoulder. Only my dad and my American cousins called me Macy. In Katzrin everybody knew me as Meskerem.

"Please get dressed quickly. I need you to look after your sisters while Ima and I finish up the packing," he said, sitting down heavily beside me on the narrow bed. His face was red and sweaty, his thick blond hair dusty and disheveled. I could hear my sisters, Abeva and Lemlem, shrieking as they chased each other through the boxes.

"I know this must be hard for you . . ." Abba started rubbing my back, but I quickly yanked the sheet over my head and muttered angrily, "If you know it's hard for me, then why don't you just leave me alone!"

My dad said nothing more. I felt the bed move as he got up and heard him walk quietly toward the living room.

"Adise, come and talk to your daughter," he said.

I waited for my mother, thinking about all the things I wanted to say to her. Not that it would help. It's not as if I hadn't told her a million times already how totally unfair it was to make us all move because of some stupid job she got and how it was ridiculous that I couldn't just stay in Katzrin with my grandmother. But then I felt her hand gently stroking my braided hair, pulling the sheet off my face. I saw that, like me, she was crying.

"Meskerem, honey, I understand how you feel. It's hard for me to leave our home too." Her voice was soft and gentle, her beautiful dark eyes shiny with tears. "Sometimes people have to choose between

two things that they really want because they can't have both."

"I chose to stay here with Grandma," I pouted, "but *you* won't let me!"

My mother sighed heavily. "We've been through this already. You're our daughter. We love you. We want you with us. You're only eleven, too young not to be with your parents."

I'll always be only-something, I thought resentfully, but I said, "You grew up with your grandmother in Ethiopia, so why can't I grow up with my grandmother here in Katzrin?"

"Yes, I grew up with my grandmother in Ethiopia, but not because I had a choice! You know my mother's story, how she walked with her friends to Sudan to reach Israel. She couldn't take me with her. I was only a baby. She was afraid I would not survive the long and dangerous journey. It was seven years before we saw each other again, and it was so hard to make up for lost time. I could never be separated from you like that." Ima hugged me tightly.

I could see it was painful for my mom to remember, and I sensed that somehow the empty white walls and the boxes piled up in the corner made it even harder.

The silence that followed was full of her sadness and mine. Eventually, instead of continuing to resist, I got up and got dressed.

After I washed my face, I lingered in the bathroom, studying my reflection in the mirror. My almond-colored eyes, just like my mom's, stared back at me as I wondered, *How would it be, living somewhere else? Would it change me?* I shook my head violently. "No!" I said aloud as my long braids, threaded with colored beads by my grandma, clicked and danced on my shoulders.

My mom is an educational counselor. She works for Israel's Ministry of Education and manages the placement of the new immigrant Ethiopian kids in all of the public schools in the Golan Heights and the surrounding areas. People from different schools all over the country come to Katzrin to meet with her. Ima created this successful educational project, putting Ethiopian kids into regular classrooms even though they don't speak Hebrew that well and their parents are unfamiliar with what the schools expect of them. Her program helps these kids fit in and be successful.

I helped Ima design the flyer for the project. My sister Lemlem's photo was even on the front page with the caption, "Young people should know about their roots and be proud. Their culture of origin is a source of strength, not a weakness." I wasn't exactly sure what that meant, but now I'm really sorry I helped. Turns out the Ministry of Education decided to adopt my mother's project and use her ideas all over the country. She got a big promotion, and now we have to move to Herzliya.

"Good! You're up!" My dad opened the door and peeked over my shoulder. "Ima's waiting for you in the living room."

My mom was standing in the living room wearing a faded T-shirt and old jeans for the move. Her tall body was bent over trying to separate my baby sister from the small potted plant she was holding. Ima did everything so patiently, but I could see the stress lines fanning out from her eyes across her temples to her short, tightly curled hair.

"I could take them to say goodbye to Grandma," I offered. Ima smiled.

I bent to distract Abeva, and she immediately let go of the potted plant and turned to grab my beads instead. Abeva had just started walking last month. Her tiny hand grabbed mine as her chubby feet made awkward, hesitant steps, and she smiled at me, revealing two endearing dimples.

"Take me with you! Me too!" shouted Lemlem. Running toward me, she grabbed my other hand. She was wearing the new red-and-white-striped overalls Grandpa Dave had sent her from America for her fourth birthday. With her tight curls and skinny legs, she looked like a boy. Lemlem was tall for her age and very mischievous. Everybody said that she was just like me.

"Are you sure you want both of them?" Ima asked.

"Yes. We should go visit Grandma together." I insisted, marching them toward the door. I knew Grandma would be pleased to see us.

"All right." Ima smiled. "Lemlem, make sure you give Meskerem your hand when you cross the street, and come back quickly. The movers will be here soon." I balanced Abeva on my hip, took Lemlem's hand, and we set off to Grandma's house.

When we reached the park, I let Abeva slip to the ground and walk beside me. With my free hand, I ran my fingers along the wall, the hedge, and the flowers.

"What are you doing?" asked Lemlem.

"I'm memorizing how beautiful everything is here." I took a deep breath. "I want Katzrin to be inside me, no matter where I go."

Lemlem looked around us and then closed her eyes and took a deep breath, copying me. She ran her little fingers gently over the flower petals. "Now Katzrin is inside me too," she declared earnestly.

I patted her hair and smiled. "Let's go," I said.

• • •

"Grandma!" Lemlem called, running along the path into Grandma's garden. Grandma got up slowly from her garden rocking chair, stretching out both arms to hug Lemlem. I paused at the gate, Abeva straddling my hip, and looked at Grandma from a distance trying to get used to the idea of saying goodbye.

"Why are you standing there? Come in!" Grandma called, reaching out to take Abeva from me. Grandma looks a lot like my mom, except with more wrinkles and silver hair. Age has rounded her shoulders, so she's closer in height to me than my mom. Her smile made me burst into tears. I couldn't help it. The tears just kept coming, despite the fact that I never cry, not even when I split my knee open on the playground at school and needed six stitches.

"Meskerem, darling, don't cry. You're scaring the baby! You're only moving to Herzliya!" Grandma, flustered, tried to comfort me. "Wait and see, you'll be back soon for the holidays, and we'll have plenty of time together!"

I couldn't answer. All my words had melted into tears.

"But we have Katzrin inside us, remember?" Lemlem pulled my hands away from my face.

"Enough." Grandma ordered, taking us into the house. "Look. I have some presents for you." There on the table were three small packages wrapped neatly in floral paper.

"Which one is mine? I want to open it!" Lemlem jumped up and down excitedly.

"First, say thank you to Mitaeh," I said, using the Amharic word for grandma in my family's part of Ethiopia. Grandma's name was Belynesh, but dad always called her Emevete, which means "my queen" and was her respect name. In Ethiopia you call people older than you by a respect name.

"Thank you, Grandma!" Lemlem took one of the presents.

"I wrote your names on them." Grandma sat

down, placing Abeva on her lap. "Let's open Abeva's first," she said.

Abeva's gift was a pretty blue backpack. Grandma had embroidered Abeva's name in white thread on the pocket.

"That's a nice backpack," said Lemlem, impatient to open her own present.

Abeva was busy trying to eat the wrapping paper, and Grandma gently took the pieces out of her mouth and gave her the new backpack to hold, saying, with tears in her eyes, "This is for you to take to your new babysitter." Grandma looked after Abeva while our parents were at work. I suddenly wondered what she would do during the day now that we were leaving, and I wondered if Abeva would like her new babysitter.

So many changes.

"I got a backpack too!" announced Lemlem, pulling out a red bag with her name embroidered in bright yellow.

"My turn," I said and opened my present. Inside was a big white pencil case. Grandma had embroidered my name in red, yellow, and green—the colors of the Ethiopian flag.

"Oh. It's beautiful, Mitaeh. Thank you." I smiled.

I couldn't wait to show it to all my friends. I had never seen such a unique pencil case. It was so colorful and pretty.

Last year, the day before school started, Ima took me to the stationery store with two of my friends, Naama and Adi. We picked out matching pencil cases with orange elephants on the front. Of course, we kept getting them mixed up since we always sat together, and this year we all promised that we would each buy different ones. I felt a pang of sadness remembering that I wouldn't be at school with them anymore.

I hugged Grandma and tried to be cheerful. "We'll come to visit all the time!" I promised. Lemlem joined in, climbing onto Grandma's lap and asking her to make braids in her hair, just like mine.

"When your hair has grown a little, sweetness. You'd better go now. Your parents will be waiting." She passed Abeva back to me, and I put her new backpack on and settled her on my hip.

"Why don't you come with us to Herzliya, Grandma?" Lemlem asked.

Grandma sighed heavily, "I have had enough changes in my life," she said. "Now, I'm not going to walk with you. My legs hurt. And anyway, I hate goodbyes." She hugged each of us again tightly and stood in her doorway, waving as we walked down the path to the road.

• • •

When we got back home, the moving van was almost packed. Abba locked the front door, and as we were getting into our car, he gave Ima a hug. "Don't worry," he told her, "Everything will be all right. This is a small move, compared to the moves we made before."

He was talking about when they had both immigrated to Israel, Ima from Ethiopia and Abba from America. Ima smiled at him and rested her head briefly on his shoulder.

"I know we'll be all right, Mike," she said, "but it's still hard to leave, especially with my mother all on her own, I wish she would agree to come with us."

"The fact that your mother is so well settled in Katzrin is a good thing. We'll visit her, and she'll visit us," Abba reassured her. Ima realized that we were listening, and she turned and said, "I know it's hard to leave Katzrin, but think of the children who came to Israel from Ethiopia on Operation Solomon and how hard it was for them to adjust to a new country and a new language. You can come back and visit Katzrin. It's not goodbye forever."

On the way to Herzliya, I pressed my forehead against the car window remembering the day a few months ago when we found out about Operation Solomon.

• • •

"Ima, come quick!" I ran to the kitchen impatiently and pulled Ima into the living room.

"What's the matter?"

I pointed at the screen as the television newscaster announced, "In an operation unprecedented in Israel's history, the remainder of Beta Israel and the Ethiopian Jewry has been brought to Israel—15,000 men, women, and children." Ima was overjoyed. She kissed me and took my hands, and we danced together around the living room.

"They did it! They really did it!" she kept saying in complete disbelief. I saw the tears in her eyes, but she was smiling from ear to ear.

Just then, Abeva woke up. "I'll get her," I told Ima. I ran to get Abeva from her crib, and by the time I came back downstairs our house was full of happy, excited neighbors, some of them immigrants eager to see their friends and relatives.

• • •

The sound of a car horn brought me back to reality. I looked at my little sisters. Abeva, in her car seat next to me, was fast asleep. Lemlem was dozing too. It made so little difference to them, us moving. Lemlem would go to a new preschool—*big deal*—and Abeva was still just a baby.

When we reached the coastal road, Abba asked me to close the window because of the strong wind from the sea. I think we'd been driving for about two hours when I noticed that the car had slowed down a lot because of traffic. There were more and more buildings around us, and for the first time, I was sorry that I had refused to go with Abba to see our new home when he had offered weeks ago. At the time, it seemed unthinkable that we would really leave Katzrin, and I was sure they would change their minds. Now I had no idea where we were going or what our new street looked like. Eventually, we stopped next to a very tall building, and Ima turned around and announced, "This is it; we're here."

"Where?" I asked uneasily.

"Herzliya. Our new home."

"This is the new house?" Lemlem was excited. Ima nodded and unbuckled my sisters from their car seats.

"This is our new home, on the sixth floor," said Abba. I looked up the side of the building. I guessed there were about 20 floors, but later I counted 10. Around the building was a very nice garden with grass and flowers and some swings, separated from the road by a row of carefully cropped bushes.

"That's nice," Lemlem said, pointing at the garden, "but how will we get up, Abba?"

"Don't worry, there's an elevator," said Abba, popping the trunk.

• • •

I had to admit, my room was really nice, with a big window looking out over the garden behind the house. Abba asked the movers to set up my furniture right after they did Abeva's crib. Ima left all her sorting to help me find my posters. In the end, even though I was the one who wanted to be there least, my room was ready before all the others. My furniture looked strange in this new place.

I sat on my bed and looked at the special album that all my friends had autographed for my goodbye party. It had a red-and-blue cover, and on the first page it said, "To our dear Meskerem from all of us, Year 4, Class 2, Katzrin."

It must have been Naama's idea, I thought, and I imagined how she and Adi must have taken the book from house to house after school getting the kids to write in it. Or did they do it during recess while somebody distracted me?

On the second page it said,

To Meskerem, my best friend of all
Please remember to call
I will not say goodbye
That would only make me cry
I will miss you so much
Make sure to stay in touch!
Love, Naama

That probably proved that it was Naama's idea, since she was first to sign. She drew puppies across the bottom of the page. She loves animals. The next page was decorated with a border of red, green, and yellow flowers. I could have recited it by heart by now, but I read it again anyway:

To Meskerem my friend
The fun we've had will never end
You may be in another place
But I will not forget your face
So write to me, you won't be lonely
I'll always be your one and only
True friend,
Love, Adi

Naama and Adi were my best friends in Katzrin. We'd known each other since we were born. We were always in each other's houses and planned everything together. When Naama's parents were sent to Brazil for the Foreign Ministry, she stayed with us for three whole months. And last year when Adi's dad told his family he was on army reserve duty and didn't come home for months, Adi confided in me about how hard it was with him away.

When he came back and told her that he helped to bring the airlift of Ethiopian Jews to Israel, we were all so proud. Whenever they talked about Operation Solomon at school, we made sure everybody knew Adi's dad had a big part in it.

I missed them both so much already.

Chapter 2
The New Kid

It wasn't like I hadn't been to the new school before. It was nearby—just a few minutes' walk along a path leading to the main road, then a quick right, and then you reached a huge building three times the size of my old school in Katzrin with classrooms all over the place, a soccer field, and a science laboratory. I hoped I wouldn't get lost on my first day. A week before school started, I went there with my dad to register. I met the principal, Edna, and my fifth grade teacher, Ariella. They seemed friendly enough. But what would the kids be like?

On the morning of my first day at school, I sat at the kitchen table, trying to choke down a few bites of cold cereal while my mother rebraided parts of my hair.

"Ima, my stomach is killing me," I whispered.

"It's okay to be a little nervous, honey. Don't worry, everything will be all right," she reassured me. Abba came back from the store with fresh rolls and made sandwiches for me and Lemlem.

"Who's taking me to my new preschool?" asked Lemlem.

"I am," said Ima, adding a final bead and surveying my fresh braids with satisfaction. I lifted my gaze to meet Abba's blue eyes.

"I'll walk with Macy," he said.

"I can walk on my own." I looked away.

"I know you can, but I'd like to walk with you." Abba handed me my lunch. "Trust me, Macy, you're a great kid. Just be yourself and everybody will want to be your friend, you'll see." Dad tried to make conversation on the way, but I was so nervous I felt like I was going to throw up if I opened my mouth.

On the other side of the road I could see kids my age walking in groups to school. None of the others were with their parents. I quickly let go of my dad's hand.

"It's all right, Abba, I can take it from here," I said.

"Are you sure?" Abba hesitated.

"Yes, no problem. See you later." I said firmly.

"All right, then. Have a good day." Abba smiled at me a little sadly but left me to continue walking on my own.

"Look at that Ethiopian, that kid—you see her?"

"Check it out. She's Ethiopian!"

I overheard some kids behind me talking as I walked up the steps into my new school. I looked around, but I didn't see anyone nearby who looked Ethiopian. It felt like all the kids were staring at me, and I told myself to relax. I heard more whispering, and a few seconds later, when I noticed a kid pointing right at me, I suddenly realized that they meant *me*.

I was the Ethiopian.

A girl with long hair pulled back into a messy ponytail appeared in front of me, hands on her hips, blocking my path through the school entrance. "When did you come to Israel?" she asked.

"Don't be silly, Sarah, she doesn't know Hebrew," someone else said behind me.

"What's your name?" asked the girl in front of me, this time in heavily accented English. Her brown eyes narrowed as she stared at me, expecting an answer.

“Back off, you’re scaring her!” A short, chubby girl with bright green eyes smiled at me encouragingly.

“Be quiet, Helen,” snapped the girl called Sarah. “Seriously. I just asked her what her name was.”

“I speak Hebrew,” I mumbled, wishing that the ground would open up and swallow me.

Somebody clapped their hands as if I had performed a trick or something.

“Good, good, she speaks Hebrew,” repeated a red-haired boy covered in freckles.

“Were you on Operation Solomon? I saw it on TV!” a boy nearby shouted. “I saw them bringing all you people in great big planes with no seats.”

"Can I touch your hair?" A kid reached for my braids.

Another tugged at my brand-new shirt. "Bet you got that at the airport. I saw how you got here on TV. You didn't bring anything with you, did you?"

"Yes, I saw that too. They had to give them all new clothes."

I blushed and stuttered. "I'm not a new immigrant!"

"Sure, you're not." Helen grinned. "My mom says that as soon as the Ethiopians got here they all became Israeli."

"Shut up, you idiot, you don't know anything," said Sarah scornfully. Then she turned to me: "We can all see that you're a new immigrant. What class did they put you in?"

"You didn't even have schools in Ethiopia, did you?"

"So, they'll put her in first grade!" The kids all snickered.

"I'm not from Ethiopia!" I shouted. They all fell silent. I hung my head. I just said that to shut them up, without even thinking about it. In a way it was true, and in a way it wasn't.

"What do you mean, you're not from Ethiopia?"

"But you're black!"

"And your hair, the braids . . ."

I searched desperately for an answer that might satisfy them, and then I had it. "I'm from America," I said.

"You mean you're African American?" The children looked at me, wide-eyed.

"Do you speak English, then?" asked Helen.

"Of course she does, stupid. If she comes from America, then she speaks English!" answered the red-haired boy. They all took a step closer.

"Have you ever been to Disneyland?"

"Do you know Michael Jackson?"

Sarah announced suddenly, "I don't believe her; she's lying!"

"Her clothes do look American. Who gives clothes like that to Ethiopians?"

"And her sneakers—look—they're Nike!"

They went on and on. I wanted to shrink into the floor and disappear as everyone offered their opinions about the American qualities of my hair, my skin, and my clothes. This was turning into the worst day of my life.

Finally, I was saved by the bell. They all scattered for their classrooms. I stood for a moment, gathering my strength, filled with regret at my decision not to allow Abba to walk all the way with me. If they'd seen Abba, they would have believed me!

• • •

My new teacher, Ariella, stood at the entrance of my classroom wearing a bright blue dress and flat sandals. She waited for me to come in and find a place to sit down, smiling at me in a friendly way. I did not feel like smiling back.

"As you can see, we have a new student in our class. Welcome," said Ariella. Everybody stared as Ariella turned to me and said kindly, "Would you like to introduce yourself?" I squirmed, uncertain. Only a week ago, when I met her with Abba, we registered me as Meskerem.

"I'm Macy," I muttered. *Abba calls me Macy. Why couldn't I use that name at school?* I thought. "My name is Macy," I lifted my voice, avoiding Ariella's gaze.

The lesson began, and we were asked to take out our notebooks and pencils. I froze. My pencil case, the one that Grandma had so carefully embroidered with my name, would immediately give me away!

"Excuse me," I said to the girl next to me, "Do you have an extra pencil? I forgot my pencil case."

• • •

When I finally got home, I took out my pencil case and threw it across the room. Looking at it, on the floor of my bedroom, I was suddenly filled with a deep sadness. I felt ashamed, as if I had somehow offended Grandma. *This is ridiculous*, I told myself angrily. *All I did was use my other name at school! So, I'm not from America, but I'm not from Ethiopia either! Let those stupid kids think whatever they want. What do I care!*

But when my gaze rested on the embroidered letters that spelled "Meskerem" in red, yellow, and green, I was once more overcome with sadness and shame. I shoved the pencil case angrily into my drawer. It was only a stupid pencil case, after all!

• • •

"How was your first day at school, Macy?" Abba asked me at dinner.

"All right," I mumbled without looking at him.

I felt Ima and Abba exchanging glances.

"Why don't you ask how my day was?" asked Lemlem.

"Because I picked you up, remember?!" Abba bent his head and rubbed noses with Lemlem, who giggled.

"Ah ba-ba-ba-ba," garbled Abeva, like she was trying to participate in the conversation. Ima fed her another spoonful of soup.

"How was your new job?" I asked Ima, trying to change the subject.

"Good, it was good," Ima smiled. "I'm preparing my big presentation for the annual Principals' Conference. I'll be working on the speech from home, but from next week on, I'll need your help with the little ones. I thought maybe tomorrow I could meet you at school and we could walk together to Lemlem's preschool. When I'm at work, I'll need you to pick her up after school and bring her home."

"No!" I exclaimed, much too loudly, and Ima looked startled by my refusal. "I mean . . . sure, of course. Only it would be better if I walked with you in the morning. You can show me then."

"All right," Ima nodded, her expression puzzled.

I hurried to clear my plate before she could ask me any more questions.

"Don't you want to tell us about school?" asked Abba as I got up, adding, "You didn't finish your food."

"I'm done eating," I answered him abruptly. Then I took the telephone into my room and shut the door.

"Adi?"

"Meskerem! How are you? It's so good to hear from you!" The sound of her voice filled me with longing.

"I'm all right. How are you?"

"All right, but we miss you!"

"How's school? Anyone new this year?

"Yes, these two boys who came over on Operation Solomon. My dad brought their families over to Katzrin. I keep checking, but nobody's moved into your old house yet. And our class got Deborah as a teacher this year—she's super strict. Today she wouldn't let Noam back in after the bell rang. He had to get a note from the principal!" I relaxed for the first time that day and let Adi's chatter wash over me in a friendly flood.

"How's your new school?" Adi was asking me.

I hesitated. What could I say?

"Meskerem, are you there?"

"Yes, yes . . . the new school is . . . nice . . ." I lied. "I'll call you tomorrow, all right?"

"Okay, I'll talk to you soon!"

"Say hello to Naama and everybody for me."

"All right, I will."

I brought the phone back to the living room, feeling better after talking to Adi. It occurred to me that tomorrow was a new day. Maybe things would get better. Tomorrow I would just go to school and tell everybody that I am Meskerem, born and raised in the Golan Heights. There was no reason not to. After all, I never planned to lie. It just happened because of all those kids with their dumb questions and the pushing and shouting. Tomorrow I would be ready.

Tomorrow I would begin again with the truth.

I smiled and went to take a shower.

Chapter 3
Macy

The next day I got up quickly and got ready for school. Ima and Abba smiled at each other, misunderstanding my eagerness. They probably thought I was excited to get to school because yesterday went so well. The truth was, I was just anxious to clear things up with the other kids and go back to being Meskerem from Katzrin, not Macy from America.

When I reached the school, I spotted a couple of kids I recognized from my class yesterday. "Hi," I said hopefully. The tall one with the messy ponytail, Sarah, looked up from her animated conversation with Helen.

"Oh, it's Macy, the American," she said sarcastically. "I was wondering, when did you make aliyah and move to Israel?"

"Actually, I was born here," I almost whispered.

"Are you kidding me? Every day a different story!" Sarah almost spat at me. She turned to the others and said, "Ignore her. She's just a liar!"

"But it's the truth," I mumbled miserably.

"Well, if you were born here, how come you know English so well? We heard you yesterday in English class!" said Gadi.

"People like *you* weren't born here," added Helen.

"What do you mean by . . . people like me?" I asked, confused.

"You know what we mean. Black Jews come from Ethiopia," Gadi stated.

"Maybe she's not even Jewish. Maybe she's just black!" Sarah scowled at me.

"I *am* Jewish!" I cried and turned and walked away as fast as I could. The last thing I needed now was to burst into tears in front of those horrible kids. I was furious! How dare they!

My desire to tell them the truth had faded and gone.

During recess, I hung out in the pet corner with two white rabbits, three hamsters, and a blue-and-yellow cockatoo. Ariella showed me where they kept the food and how to clean the cages and left me to it. I was happy to keep busy in the pet corner. I did not even want to look at the kids in my class.

• • •

When I got back from school, I went to my room and opened my closet. I took out the two white embroidered shirts that Adi's dad had brought me from Addis Ababa and hid them under some old jeans. From now on, I would wear the colorful printed tees from New York and Miami that Grandpa Dave had sent me for my last birthday. I folded the pretty white dress Grandma had made for me, with the carefully

embroidered blue stars of David. I didn't like wearing dresses, anyway. Then I took my box of hair accessories and removed all the green, yellow, and red ones I had so keenly collected last year. I was busy trying to erase the name Meskerem from my art folder when my mother came into the room and asked, "What are you up to?"

I jumped.

"Nothing." I tried to act casual, flipping over the art folder so that she wouldn't see what I had done.

"I'm going shopping. Want to come with me?" asked Ima. Usually I love shopping with my mother. She's always so busy, it's fun to be alone with her and talk about things. But now all I could think about was what would happen if the kids from my class saw me with her. What would they think?

For a second I thought of pretending that she wasn't my mom if we bumped into them . . . It seemed easier just to stay at home.

"No, Ima, I'm not in the mood. I could look after Lemlem and Abeva for you," I offered, trying to be helpful.

"That's nice of you, but I'd rather you came with me. We could talk on the way. I don't see enough of you lately." Ima smiled at me, and she came closer to stroke my hair. I hurriedly slipped the art folder down between the bed and the wall and squirmed away from her hand.

"I don't want to go," I said grumpily.

But instead of leaving, Ima sat down on the edge of my bed and asked gently, "What's the matter, Meskerem? You know you can talk to me."

I looked away miserably and didn't answer.

"You know you can tell me anything, anything at all," Ima tried again, stroking my arm. Suddenly, I was angry—furious. I wanted her to leave me alone. I wanted her to somehow understand without me having to explain, because there was no way I could put into words what was going on.

"I can't tell you!" I shouted at her, tears streaming down my cheeks, "You don't understand anything!" I ran out of the room, leaving her gaping at me in surprise, a good, considerate mother with a bad liar for a daughter.

I ran out of the apartment and down the stairs, afraid I might bump into Abba if I took the elevator. I kept running until I got to the park on our corner. I sat on a swing. Where could I go? In Katzrin I would have gone straight to Grandma's house, but here I had no one. I was just too far from home.

I started undoing my braids, pulling at my hair till it hurt. I hated myself. I threw the colored beads into the bushes. When the mosquitoes started biting, I walked home slowly.

When I got back Abba tried to talk to me, but I told him I wanted to go to sleep.

Chapter 4
Games

The next few days passed slowly. None of the kids spoke to me. I spoke to no one. Much to Ima's dismay, I refused to let her rebraid my hair, so it hung wild around my shoulders. I spent recess with the rabbits, hamsters, and cockatoo.

On the day of my mother's conference, I picked up Lemlem from preschool. When I left school, I had the feeling I was being followed. I could hear kids behind me whispering and giggling. The preschool gate was open, and I hurried to find Lemlem.

"Listen, I want you to play a game with me," I told her as she put on her little red backpack.

"What game?" Lemlem beamed at me, excited.

"When we walk home, let's pretend that we are in our own private world. If anyone talks to us or asks any questions, let's pretend that they don't exist and not answer them."

Lemlem pulled a face. "That's not a game!"

I looked at her. She was just too smart to fall for that. "It'll be fun," I tried to convince her.

"All right," said Lemlem, "but only if you promise to play with me when we get home."

"It's a deal."

As I'd expected, the kids who had been following me were waiting for us. I took Lemlem's hand firmly in mine and marched her toward home.

"Hey, you, Macy's brother, come here a minute." I recognized Gadi's voice.

"Say, little brown boy, what's your name?" Helen called out.

"I'm a girl!" Lemlem turned and scowled at them. I pulled her hand, reminding her that she had promised not to talk to them. I wanted to laugh. Lemlem was annoyed at being called a boy but not at being called little or brown.

"Little girl, Macy's sister, what's your name?" Lemlem tightened her grip on my hand and walked quietly beside me. I prayed that they would leave us alone. I really didn't want them to know where I lived.

"Why are you running away? Do you think you're too good to talk to us?" Sarah did not sound friendly.

"Black snobs!" someone snorted.

I had had enough. I ducked into a nearby apartment building, pretending it was ours, and waited in the stairwell, hoping they would leave.

Lemlem hid quietly with me for a few minutes, and then I asked her softly, "Please don't tell Ima and Abba what happened, okay?"

Lemlem nodded and squeezed my hand. When we finally got home, I heated up our lunch and spent the rest of the afternoon playing board games with Lemlem.

Abba called to check up on us and to tell us that he and Abeva had just picked Ima up. "We'll be home soon, honey. Please make sure you do your homework."

"Can I talk to Ima?" I asked. "I want to hear about the conference."

"Wait till we get home," Abba said abruptly. "See you soon."

When they came back I watched sullenly as Ima hugged Lemlem and kissed Abeva before handing her over to Abba for her shower. Ima's hair was combed into a perfect cropped Afro, and she wore a new, dark red outfit she had bought especially for the occasion. I always admired the way she looked, naturally beautiful without any makeup, her face lit up by her smile. But now she looked drawn and exhausted.

"How was the conference, Ima?"

She looked at me and smiled cheerlessly. "Thank you for looking after Lemlem today. How did it go?"

"It was fine, Ima. But what about the conference? Did they like your project?"

"It's done," Ima sighed heavily "Go to bed, sweetie."

I went to my room, convinced that she was still angry with me.

That night I couldn't sleep. I kept thinking about going back to school and dreading the morning. I crept out of bed to get a glass of water, and I heard my parents' conversation, loud for so late at night, drifting through their open bedroom door. My mother's voice sounded so hurt that I stopped short. I couldn't help listening.

". . . literally, a sea of white faces. I was the only black person in the room. He introduced me as 'the interpreter who works with our Ethiopian families.'

He actually said, 'In a few moments the expert on early childhood education who spearheaded the project will arrive and present it.' As if a black woman couldn't be an expert in early childhood education! I just can't believe the chairman of the education department thought I was the interpreter. How humiliating!"

I was stunned. What was she talking about?

"I almost died. But I got up and said, 'The expert on early childhood education who spearheaded the project is right here. I was not aware that you also invited an interpreter, but apparently she hasn't arrived yet.' And I sailed right into my presentation. You could have heard a pin drop. The chairman almost swallowed his tongue in shame."

I could hear my dad start comforting her before he closed the bedroom door. Luckily, he didn't see me. I hurried back to bed, my thoughts racing.

Chapter 5
Hiding

Behind our new home there was a playground with a sandbox and some swings on a neat patch of grass. It was nothing like the old playground in Katzrin, which had an enormous climbing structure with wooden frames and thick hanging ropes. The kids always raced each other to climb to the top. With my long legs and strong arms, I was always among the fastest, even faster than most of the boys. Adi and Naama and all our friends used to meet up there, sitting on the ground below or hanging from the ropes for hours, just talking. I wished I was back there now as I sat on the grass, watching Lemlem in the sandbox.

"Come and play with me," she said for the umpteenth time.

"I don't feel like it," I said impatiently.

She looked up at me with huge dark eyes and asked seriously, "How come you're so sad?"

"I'm not sad, Lemlem. What makes you think I'm sad?" I forced a smile. I was surprised that she had even noticed.

"You are sad," my little sister insisted, "I can tell." She dumped out the sand in her bucket and added, "In Katzrin you used to play with me, but here you always hurry to bring me straight home from preschool. And you never take me out exploring like you used to. Are you mad at me?"

My heart melted. I stroked her curly hair and said, "I'm not mad at you. I just hate school here. I miss Katzrin."

"Mes-kerem, Lem-lem," I heard my mom shouting from the window. I looked at my watch and saw that we were late for dinner. I quickly rose and brushed the sand from my lap, pulling Lemlem along with me, when suddenly, from the corner of my eye, I saw Sarah and Gadi with two other kids I recognized from school. They were dressed in their youth group uniforms and coming out of the building next door. They were looking up at our building.

"Look at that Ethiopian woman shouting her

head off from the window!" I heard one of the kids say, I couldn't tell which one.

I froze in my tracks.

"Mes-kerem, Lem-lem!" *Why did she have to shout like that?* I grabbed Lemlem and hid behind the slide, putting my hand over her mouth before she had a chance to shout back to Ima.

"What strange names," laughed one of the girls.

"Why are you shouting from the window? This isn't the jungle!" called another. I hung my head, praying that they wouldn't see us. From where we were hiding I couldn't actually see the kids, but I could hear them.

"Mi-sir-cream, Lema-lema-lem" they mimicked. Lemlem tried to push my hand away from her face, but I held tight, determined to remain hidden until they passed. Only when I was sure the coast was clear did I let go. I apologized, but Lemlem pushed me away and ran home crying.

"Lemlem, wait," I called, "You forgot your toys in the sandbox. Come back, I'll help you with them."

"Why did you close my mouth?" she whimpered.

"I'm sorry, Lemlem. I'm really, really sorry. I'll never do it again. Here, I'll help you carry your toys, and we'll go home together. Please don't tell Ima, okay?"

When we stepped out of the elevator Ima was standing there, about to come look for us. "You're late! I was calling and calling you! I made omelets and fries, and it's all getting cold!" she scolded. "Get inside! Here I am calling and calling, and you don't even answer!"

"Why do you have to shout our names from the window? Are you stupid or something?!" I shouted back at her and slammed the door.

Ima looked horrified. I had never spoken to her like that before. Even Lemlem froze, speechless. I hung my head, waiting for a punishment. But my mom never raised a hand to us and rarely raised her voice in anger, and she didn't now. She just stood there staring at me, her eyes full of sadness.

After what seemed like forever, she said gently, "Meskerem, this way of talking is not acceptable. When you would like to discuss what is bothering you, you will find me in the kitchen."

I ran to my room, closed the door, and threw myself down on the bed. I was so ashamed. How could I yell at Ima like that? How could I ever face her again? *She'll never forgive me*, I thought. That night

I didn't leave my room. Abba came to try to talk to me, but I didn't answer him. I fell asleep early, still in my clothes.

As the first rays of sunlight touched my window in the morning, I woke with a start, remembering last night. I washed my face and brushed my teeth, and then somehow my feet found their way into my parents' room, where I curled up next to Ima.

"It's okay. I love you, sweetie," Ima reassured me sleepily and hugged me close. "We all make mistakes sometimes." But the tears kept rolling down my cheeks. I could not forgive myself. I wished I could tell her everything, about all the lies I had told at school about not being Ethiopian. But the words wouldn't come.

Chapter 6
Roots

The next morning at school Ariella held up a big picture of a tree and said, "If we compared our families to this tree, who would be the roots? The trunk? The branches? The flowers?"

If a tree symbolized my family, I thought, then the roots would be Grandma in Katzrin and Grandpa in America. I looked at the picture Ariella was holding. The roots were thick ropes stretching deep into the earth. If the roots are the grandparents, I thought, then the trunk must be the parents, and the flowers are the children. But I didn't raise my hand. I knew that if I did, thirty-seven pairs of unfriendly eyes would turn toward me.

A bubbly, blue-eyed girl named Shira raised her hand, pointed at the roots, and said, "Those symbolize grandparents."

"Very good!" said Ariella, "Like a tree, a family grows from its roots, the family ancestors. Over the next few weeks we will examine our own roots and each one of you will prepare your very own family tree. I want each one of you to start thinking about how to draw your own family tree. Talk to your parents, your aunts and uncles, and grandparents! Ask them to tell you about where your families are from."

Then Ariella handed out copies of the president's family tree. Under each name, there was a description of where and when that person was born. I stared at the diagram in front of me and wondered how exactly I was supposed to get through this assignment.

That very afternoon, I worked on my family tree. I started with Grandpa Dave in America. Grandpa Dave is wiry and tall and has wild, bushy white hair. He likes us to call him Dave instead of Grandpa. He always sends us presents on our birthdays and for Hanukkah, but because he lives so far away, I've only met him four times in my entire life. The last time I saw him was two years ago, right after Grandma Rose died, and he was very sad.

I try to remember Grandma Rose. I can almost

see her surrounded by all her grandchildren, dishing out freshly made cupcakes. I can't quite picture her face, but I can hear her hoarse voice calling me "Shayna maidel, my beautiful girl." All the furniture in their house was covered in lace doilies, and when I was a baby, my favorite blanket was a pink-and-white knitted afghan that Grandma Rose sent me.

My thoughts wandered to my grandma in Katzrin. I saw her every day for almost my whole life until we moved here. Ever since I could remember, I spent hours at her house, every day. She's lived there for years; she settled there just after she arrived in Israel.

Grandma escaped from Ethiopia during the civil war with a group of young people, including my grandfather. I never met my mom's father because he was killed by robbers on that journey, long before I was born. He was a real hero. Grandma told me that to get from Ethiopia to the Sudan, they had to cross a jungle to avoid the soldiers patrolling the border. The group had hired a guide, but he tricked them and led them straight into an ambush. The robbers attacked them and took everything, but when they tried to kidnap the women, my grandfather and the other men in the group protected them. There was a terrible fight, and the women escaped into the darkness.

Grandma hid in the bushes for two days, afraid to come out, waiting for the men to come back. On the third day the women left their hiding places and returned to the scene of the fight. They found my grandpa, dead. He was only twenty-three years old. There's a picture of Grandpa on the wall in Grandma's house.

Grandma told me that when they set out for Israel, they left my two-year-old mother with Grandma's parents in the village. She said that in Ethiopia it was common for grandparents to raise their grandchildren, since most women married and had children when they were still very young. Grandma was only fifteen when my mom was born. When she left Ethiopia, they believed the planes would come soon and take all the Jews to Israel. But when Grandma finally arrived in Israel alone after a dangerous two-year journey, she discovered that things were more complicated than she'd expected. She told me how in the mornings she studied Hebrew and at night she wept for the daughter she missed so much.

When she remembered those times, Grandma used to cry, saying that had she known that her husband would die and that it would take seven years to be reunited with her only daughter, she never would have left Ethiopia. When I was younger and spent all my time at Grandma's house, Ima used to say that I was making up for all the lost time between them. I loved listening to Grandma's stories and often confided in her too. Now I missed her terribly.

Chapter 7

Birthday

"Macy, what would you like to do for your birthday?" Ima and Abba asked.

"To visit Grandma," I answered, without hesitation.

Everything was planned. We would leave after school on Thursday for a visit that would last until Saturday evening. I couldn't wait!

But then, everything went wrong.

On the Wednesday before my birthday Abeva woke up with a very high temperature. What bad luck! Still, Ima felt bad for me and tried to make it work.

"Don't worry, Meskerem, I'll stay with Abeva, and you and Lemlem can go with Abba to Katzrin," Ima reassured me.

But the next day, on Thursday morning, just as Lemlem and I were about to go to school, the phone rang.

"Oh! Oh no!" Ima exclaimed, holding the phone and raising her hand to cover her mouth in shock. She was shaking. I froze with my hand on the door-knob, Lemlem right behind me.

"What hospital?" Ima was asking, biting her lip. We rushed back to stand beside her. She wrote down some information and hung up the phone, sinking heavily into a kitchen chair. Lemlem and I waited impatiently for her to tell us what had happened.

"Abba was in a car accident," Ima said finally, "but he's all right, thank God."

"So why is he in the hospital?" I asked. Lemlem burst into tears.

"Don't cry; he's okay." Ima hugged her. "Abba's in the hospital for some tests, and hopefully, he'll be released soon." Ima forced a smile and wiped away Lemlem's tears.

I put down my schoolbag and helped Lemlem take off hers.

"What are you doing?" asked Ima.

"We'll wait here for Abba," I said.

"No, Meskerem." Ima handed me Lemlem's back-pack. "You'll take Lemlem to preschool and go to school. Trust me, Abba is all right. There's no point in missing school. You will see him when you get home."

"But, Ima . . ." I protested.

"No buts," she interrupted me firmly. We did as we were told.

• • •

When we got home from school, Abba was already there. He was lying on the sofa looking quite pale, with a big white bandage wrapped around his left arm, which was hanging in a sling tied around his neck. I kissed his forehead gently and sat down beside him on the floor.

"How are you feeling, Abba?"

"Don't worry, Macy. I'm all right."

"Does it hurt, Abba?" asked Lemlem.

"Only when I laugh," joked Abba. "My shoulder was dislocated; it's really tender."

"What happened?" I asked.

"Another driver drove into my car at the intersection. He was in too much of a hurry and ran the light."

Just then, Ima came in with drinks and said seriously, "Meskerem, I'm so sorry, but we're going to have to put off our trip to Katzrin."

"I'm sorry too. I know how much you've been

looking forward to it," added Abba, reaching for me with his free hand.

"It's all right, Abba." I forced a smile. "I'm glad you are okay. Maybe Grandma can come and visit us?"

"We've already suggested that, but she doesn't feel well enough to travel."

"It's okay, I can wait until next weekend," I said, shrugging my shoulders. I caught Ima and Abba exchanging glances, and I knew there was more bad news coming.

"Honey, the car is totaled." Abba said softly. I was shocked. All my birthday plans, ruined! No Katzrin this weekend or next weekend . . . who knew when we would be able to go?

This was too much. I tried to be happy because Abba was all right, and that was what really mattered. But I couldn't help it—I was furious. Even on my birthday, I couldn't get what I wanted.

I turned and ran out of the room, slamming the door. Nothing was going my way. I flung myself onto my bed as the tears started coming. From the hallway I heard my dad say, "Poor thing. Her birthday is ruined. Maybe we should just send her to Katzrin by bus, if she wants to go so much." I perked up, listening.

"Mike, are you joking? She's not yet twelve years old! Alone? She would have to change buses about three times!"

I sighed heavily and sank back into my pillow. It was hopeless.

"Why three?" Abba was asking.

"From Herzliya to Tel Aviv, from Tel Aviv to Tiberias, and from Tiberias to Katzrin!" Ima sounded irritated.

"Adise," said Abba, calmly, "Line 843 leaves Tel Aviv once a day, at 9 a.m., straight to Katzrin. She wouldn't have to change buses at all."

"How do you know? How long have you been thinking about this crazy idea without telling me?"

Abba sighed. "I called the bus company after your mother said she couldn't come. Think about it. You know Macy is a very reliable girl."

"I know that our daughter is responsible, but what about everyone else? Don't you listen to the news? I will not have my little girl traveling across the country on buses! She can wait a couple of weeks to visit Katzrin."

"It's not a matter of a couple of weeks, Adise, and you know it," Abba continued to argue. I couldn't believe he understood how urgent this was for me, and I was surprised to hear him say, "Macy has been waiting for this visit for a long time. It's not that complicated to travel from Herzliya to Tel Aviv and then get a bus directly to Katzrin."

"Mike!" my mom's voice was steel. "I can't believe that you're serious! Maybe you banged your head in that accident!"

This time, Abba didn't answer, and I knew he'd given up. But my tears had dried. All I had to do was get a bus to Tel Aviv and then take line 843 all the way to Katzrin.

• • •

In the morning I pretended to prepare for school as usual, but instead of my schoolbooks, I put a change of clothes, my wallet, and some snacks in my bag. I could tell that Ima and Abba were being extra nice to me. I smiled and pretended that I was all right. I took Lemlem to preschool and watched the stream of children entering my own school. Then I hurried to catch the bus to the central station in Tel Aviv. I was worried that it would take me too long to find bus number 843 and I would miss the only bus to Katzrin.

I asked the bus driver what platform I needed, and he told me where to go. The Tel Aviv bus station looked like a giant mall, but I did not stop to look at the shop windows. I went straight to the platform to catch my bus to Katzrin.

I bought a ticket from the driver and sat down at the window, my heart racing like a thousand beating drums. I remembered the car ride from Katzrin to Herzliya when we first moved. It was a long drive. I was filled with a mixture of excitement and apprehension. In just a few hours (alone on this bus full of strangers!) I would see my grandma and Katzrin! The bus was filling up.

Someone asked if the seat next to me was empty. I nodded, and a young soldier sat beside me. His hair was cropped so short you could see his scalp. He pushed his duffel bag into the luggage rack, put his gun on his lap, and offered me a piece of chocolate as he sat down.

"Want some?"

I shook my head. My family had taught me not to speak to strangers. Finally, the bus pulled out of the station and we were on our way. The soldier looked around and then asked, "Are you traveling by yourself?"

"Why are you talking to me? I don't know you!" I stammered and turned away, looking out the window.

"Sorry." The soldier smiled at me. "I never met a girl who didn't like chocolate before." He broke a piece off the bar and offered it to me.

I hesitated. "No, thank you."

"You know, you remind me of my little sister. She's shy too. By the way, my name is Dekel." He offered me his strong hand, and I shook it.

"I'm Mesk . . . Macy. And I'm not shy," I said. The soldier was only being nice. Suddenly, I wanted

to talk to him. "I'm going to visit my grandma in Katzrin."

"So we have a long journey together." The soldier smiled again, then leaned back and closed his eyes. I looked out of the window, thinking about school starting without me and wondered if anyone would notice that I wasn't there. I reminded myself to keep track of the time, to call home before I was supposed to come back from school. I didn't want them to worry about me. Suddenly, my stomach began to ache. Maybe it was the thought of my parents waiting for me at home or perhaps the excitement at finally being on my way to Katzrin. I folded my arms over my stomach and glanced at the soldier next to me. He was already asleep, but his presence reassured me. He looked so capable. I leaned back and closed my eyes too.

Chapter 8
Grandma

When I woke up I could see the Sea of Galilee from the window. The soldier was listening to music through his earphones, and behind us two women were chattering in a foreign language. I stretched and waited impatiently to reach Katzrin.

Dekel got off the bus at Tiberias, and I was left alone. As the bus climbed the hills toward the Golan, my excitement grew, imagining how surprised and pleased Grandma would be to see me.

I got off at the museum in Katzrin and ran all the way to Grandma's house. She was sitting on her porch swing.

"Mitaeh!"

"Meskerem? I can't believe it! I'm sitting here thinking about you on your birthday, and God sent you to me!"

I laughed and embraced her with all my strength.

"You're so big," she said. "And where are your beautiful braids?"

"How are you, Grandma?" I asked, suddenly shy. I could see that her legs were swollen.

"I'm fine, aside from missing my grandchildren. Where is everybody?" She glanced toward the road, as if expecting Ima and Abba to appear with Lemlem and Abeva.

"I came by myself," I confessed, looking down at the ground. Grandma looked at me quizzically, so I said, "It's a long story, and I'm thirsty."

"Go and get us some lemonade from the fridge," said Grandma. When I came back with two frosty glasses, she patted the seat next to her and said firmly, "Now sit down and tell me how you got here."

I started talking, and Grandma sat and listened. Sometimes she nodded and sighed, and when she heard about that day with Lemlem at the park, she shook her head sadly, stroking my wild hair. But she never once stopped me and just let the words that had been bottled up all these months pour out, until I finally fell quiet. I told Grandma everything. When I finished, I felt exhausted but lighter, as if a great weight had been lifted off my chest.

"You know what you need to do now, don't you?" Grandma looked at me seriously. I nodded and went into the house to look for the telephone.

"Abba?" I'd completely lost track of the time. It was already way past the hour I was expected home from school.

"Macy! I'm so glad you called!" Abba sounded worried. "Where are you?"

"Please say you won't be mad, Abba," I trembled.

"What happened?" said Abba anxiously.

"Abba, I'm with Grandma. In Katzrin."

There was a long silence.

"Abba?"

"You're joking, right?"

"No, Abba, I took the bus. Instead of going to school . . ." My voice trailed off.

There was a long silence on the other end.

"Macy, sweetie, are you okay?"

"I'm okay, Abba. I had to come. I just had to . . . I'm sorry."

"I know, Macy. Well. I'm relieved that I know where you are and that you are all right," Abba said. He didn't sound angry. "Sweetness, we'll talk again later, okay? I want to call Ima and let her know where you are. She's been very worried."

"Thanks, Abba."

I hung up the phone and breathed a sigh of relief. *How lucky I am to have such an understanding dad,* I thought. I knew that Ima would eventually understand too, at least when she got over being mad at me.

I went back to Grandma and said, "I don't know what to do. I made such a mess of things with my story about being from America, and I hate those kids! They keep bothering me all the time. You have to help me convince Ima and Abba to let me stay here with you."

Grandma took my hands in hers and said, "Meskerem, you know perfectly well that your mother would never agree to that. Anyhow, it's never a good thing to run away from your problems."

Tears filled my eyes. "I don't know how to solve this," I wailed. "I can't deal with those kids. They're horrible. They hate me. I tried telling them the truth, but they won't believe me! I wish there was magic that would make them like me. I wish I could have friends there like I do here . . ."

Grandma said gently "Maybe there is magic that can do that." I looked up at her to see if she was kidding, but her face was serious.

"What do you mean?" I asked, curious.

"Sit down." Grandma indicated the ground at her feet and spread her knees so that I could sit between them. "I braid, and you listen," she ordered, taking hold of my hair. Listening to her soothing voice, with her clever hands braiding my hair, I calmed down. It felt like the simple days before the move.

"Years ago, there lived in Ethiopia a woman who was married to a man who was unhappy with her," Grandma began in her rhythmic storytelling voice. "They were always quarreling, and nothing she did could please him. The woman was miserable. She didn't know what to do. So she went to the local magician. 'Please give me a love potion that will return my husband's love for me,' said the woman. The magician answered, 'Bring me three whiskers from a lion and I will give you the love potion.'

"The woman returned home, feeling hopeless. How could she possibly get three whiskers from a lion without being eaten? But her desire to improve her marriage motivated her to try. She lay awake every night until she thought of a plan. She went to a neighbor and asked him to kill her a sheep. Then she cut up the meat, put it in a large sack, and went out into the jungle to look for a lion. She climbed a tree and waited.

"After a few hours, a lion appeared, lured by the smell of the fresh meat. The woman threw him a large piece from her sack. The lion ate the meat hungrily and padded away silently, back into the forest. The woman climbed down from the tree and headed home.

"The next day, the woman again took her sack to the forest and climbed up the same tree. Only this time, she sat on a lower branch. When the lion appeared, she threw him a piece of meat, just like before, and the lion ate it. Encouraged, the next day the woman moved still closer to the lion as she fed him and still closer with each passing day. When a month had gone by, she had him eating from the palm of her hand. She reached out and stroked the lion's face, gently pulling out three white whiskers. Then the woman gave the lion the remainder of the meat and went happily home.

"The very next day she went back to the magician. 'So,' he asked her, 'did you bring me three lion's whiskers?'

"'Yes, I did,' said the woman proudly, 'and here they are!' The woman stretched out her hand and showed the magician the lion's whiskers.

"'How did you manage to do that?' asked the magician, amazed. The woman told him how for a month she had fed the lion, first from the tree and then from the ground, until he had willingly eaten from the palm of her hand.

"'Now, give me the love potion you promised me,' she said.

"'You don't need it,' the magician replied.

"'What do you mean?'" exclaimed the woman. 'After all I've done you won't give me the love potion?'

"The magician smiled at the woman kindly and said, 'You don't need any love potions or magic spells. After all the courageous efforts you made to get close to a wild lion, I am certain that you will be able, with far less effort, to get close to your husband and rekindle his love.'

"The woman walked home slowly, the magician's words in her head and her heart. She went back to her husband full of confidence after having tamed a wild lion, and in time, she discovered that the magician was right."

Grandma smoothed my newly braided hair. For a long time I sat quietly, thinking about Grandma's story. I was thinking that it would be easier to tame a wild lion than to make friends with the kids in my class.

Grandma turned me toward her and looked into my eyes with her wise ones. As if reading my thoughts, she said, "As soon as we stop thinking of things as impossible, they become possible. After all, you got all the way out here all by yourself, didn't you?"

Chapter 9
Mom

After Friday night dinner I met up with Naama and Adi, and it was just like old times. They were really impressed that I had traveled all the way by myself on the bus. They promised to come to Herzliya together soon for a sleepover in my new room. I didn't tell them about the trouble with the kids at school, but their friendship gave me strength.

On Sunday morning I returned home by bus.

"I don't want you traveling on Saturday night. I'll meet you at the Tel Aviv bus station at 10," Ima said on the phone. I was afraid she would be really angry with me, but she just sounded resigned. I wondered if I would be in big trouble when I got back.

When the bus stopped in Tiberias, I remembered Dekel, the friendly soldier, and looked for him as the new passengers boarded, but of course, he wasn't there. All the way home I gazed out the window at the beautiful scenery, thinking about my weekend in Katzrin. It felt so much longer than just a weekend. For the first time in ages, I actually felt okay about going back to school. I knew what I had to do. Grandma's story, like magic, had paved the way forward.

When I got off the bus in Tel Aviv, I looked around for the bus stop to Herzliya. There were Abba and Ima waiting for me—Abba with his sling, Ima tall and beautiful. Their eyes lit up when they

spotted me, and I flew into their arms. They both hugged me tight. "Thank God," Ima murmured. When I saw her smile, I knew she wasn't angry anymore. Abba had to leave us to go to a meeting, so we said goodbye, and I walked with Ima.

At the corner we stopped at a local bakery. To my surprise Ima sat down at a table outside and motioned for me to join her. "Don't you have to be at work?" I asked.

"I'm having coffee with my daughter," she replied.

I smiled. As I sipped my chocolate milk, I wondered what she would say if I told her about the kids at school. I wondered what she would say if I told her that I knew that it wasn't so simple for her at work either. Now that I wasn't so angry anymore, I could see how much she loved me and how keeping the secret of my miserable school life for so many weeks had somehow changed things between us.

"Ima," I said casually, "do you have any pictures of Ethiopia?"

She looked up at me, and her face lit up as she replied, "Of course I do. I didn't think you were interested in Ethiopia. I'll show you when we get home."

• • •

At home, she opened her computer and showed me her presentation about Ethiopia and where the new immigrants had come from. I was stunned. It was such a beautiful place!

"Ima! All these green pastures and hills, the cattle and sheep grazing, the children playing . . . it looks lovely!"

Ima smiled at me. "And here is the Fasilides Castle, and this is the market in Gonder. Look at all those colorful woven baskets and all the different herbs . . ." She sighed. "You see, Meskerem, one of the problems is that people often assume things based on appearances."

I said quickly, "Like if you're black, you're an interpreter and not an expert in early childhood education?"

Ima looked stunned. "How did you know?"

"I heard you talking to Abba." I lowered my eyes. "The kids at school thought I was a new immigrant," I mumbled.

Ima nodded, understanding. "There's nothing wrong with being an interpreter or a new immigrant. It hurts when people think they know you because of how you look. The only way to overcome this is to let people know who you really are."

That first day at school came back to me: all the kids staring at me and shouting. As if she had read my thoughts, Ima said softly, "There's no escaping people's responses to our skin color. A lot of people feel uncomfortable or even afraid when they see someone who's different. That's why the children at your school were unfriendly to you."

I let her words soak in. These last few months I'd been so wrapped up in my own private world, sure that nobody could understand me, especially not my mom, and yet she was the one who would have understood me the most. I got up and hugged her. "I'm sorry, Ima."

"What for?"

I hung my head. "I didn't want the other kids to know where you came from," I confessed.

"My dear Meskerem, we have nothing to be ashamed of." She stroked my braids. Her face was serious as she stared into my eyes. At that moment I felt very close to her. "If you know for sure who you are, nobody else can determine that for you, and it doesn't matter what ugly words they use. Always remember that, because you are a lovely, special girl, and there is no reason on earth for you to feel less than anybody else."

"Ima," I blurted, relieved that she wasn't angry with me, "tell me about growing up. I'm getting a pen and paper. I want to write everything down."

I had already heard a lot about growing up in Ethiopia from Grandma, but my mom never spoke about her childhood. I only knew that she used to dream of her mother and, waking up at night alone in the dark, she would creep into her grandmother's bed and cry herself to sleep. But I never knew about her life and how she spent her days before she arrived here.

I sat beside my mom as she described the people and places of her childhood. For two hours, I listened and wrote. I regretted never asking these questions before, and I was ashamed at never taking an interest in Ima's childhood. Maybe if I had known what she had gone through, it would have helped me to understand her better.

"In the years that I was separated from my parents," Ima was saying, "there was no contact between us: no letters, no phone calls. I didn't even know if they were alive or if they had reached Israel . . . I wondered if they had a new family and had forgotten about me. Later, I discovered that my mom had written many letters that never reached our village."

"How did you get to Israel?"

"Your great-grandmother was a very kind and generous woman. I will never forget her. But the trip was too hard, and she was old, so she refused to come. I traveled with my uncle Tegavu, but when the opportunity arose he sent me ahead to Israel on a plane with a group of children."

"By yourself?!" I couldn't even imagine it. I had felt grown up just traveling to Katzrin. Suddenly, it was clear to me why my mom had always found it so hard to part from me or even let me out of her sight. "So what happened when you got here?" I asked, curious. "How did you find Grandma?"

"When I arrived, I was all alone. All of us kids were placed in temporary housing together while they looked for our families. It was so strange. People were speaking Hebrew, which I didn't understand, wearing different clothes, and there was so much food! Things I had never tasted before, like ice cream—I couldn't get enough of it!" Ima continued. "But the officials couldn't find my parents on their lists. Since I was only nine, I needed to enroll in school. One of them said they should just send me to boarding school and not to bother looking anymore, that my parents probably didn't make it over. Luckily, the interpreter refused to give up, and he insisted on going over the lists again and again, looking for my parents' names. He kept asking me questions, like if they had any other names or if I could be more specific about the exact date they left Ethiopia.

"It took a long time. I prayed with all my being that I would find my parents. I'll never forget that moment when the translator walked over with a big smile on his face, looked me right in the eyes and said, 'I think I found your mother.'

"I was so happy, I didn't even ask where my father was; I just assumed they were together. The officials sent me by taxi all the way to Katzrin from Ashkelon. I thought the journey would never end! When we reached Katzrin, my mother was waiting for me on the swing beside her house, the same swing that you and she sit on together and talk. I ran out of the taxi and fell into her arms, and we both cried and cried."

My mom was quiet. "Later, she told me my father didn't make it." She stood up. "I'll be right back," she said and left the room. She returned a minute later, holding a small box, which she handed to me. "Meskerem, this was your grandpa's. It's the only possession of his we have left. Grandma gave it to me, but I want you to have it."

"What is it?"

"Open it and see."

I opened the box carefully. Inside was a small Star of David on a chain. The Magen David was made of real gold.

"Grandpa could not wear the star in Ethiopia because it was too dangerous to be openly Jewish," Ima explained. "He kept it in his pocket and said that when he reached Israel, he would wear it with pride."

I took the necklace out and put it on. It made me feel connected to Grandpa and to both Ethiopia and Israel. "I will wear this with pride," I said. "I promise."

• • •

It was almost midnight when I finally finished my project. The next day, when I got up, I went straight to the living room table to see my family tree. It was ready. Each family name had a picture beneath. Shades of white, brown, and everything in between. Flowers, branches, trees, and roots. Grandparents, uncles, cousins.

"Wow, amazing!" Lemlem said admiringly.

"Come, wash up and come and have breakfast." My mom hurried us along.

I followed her into the kitchen. "Ima, I can't eat. My stomach hurts." I complained. She turned toward me. "You'll be fine," she said reassuringly. "I'll help you roll up the tree."

Chapter 10
Meskerem

The closer I got to school, the more my stomach ached. When I saw the kids in the playground, I had to force myself to put one foot in front of another and walk forward. I remembered Grandma's story about the brave woman feeding the lion from the palm of her hand and took a deep breath.

"Hey. Where were you yesterday?" asked Sarah. "You missed the math quiz."

"I was away for the weekend. I went to visit my grandma. I got back late yesterday." I answered.

"You flew to America for the weekend?" teased Gadi. The knot in my stomach grew tighter.

"No," I answered quietly, raising my eyes to meet his. "I took a bus to Katzrin. That's where she lives."

"Who cares where the liar was yesterday. Let's go, class is starting." Sarah spun on her heel, and they all hurried after her into the classroom. I followed slowly. Gadi lingered behind me, shooting me a questioning look as we rushed to our seats.

After the class quieted down, Ariella began to explain with great excitement that our class had been chosen to exhibit our family tree projects in the school lobby in honor of Parents Day.

"Is there anybody who wants to tell us about their project?" she asked, smiling at the class.

Here's my chance, I thought, but my mouth felt like dust and I couldn't speak.

"Me!" said Shira. She rose and walked to the front of the classroom. She seemed to have no trouble at all speaking in front of a crowd! I wished I could be like her.

"My grandmother on my mother's side comes from Poland, and my dad's family comes from Morocco. All of my grandmother's family, except Grandma, were killed in the Holocaust." She passed around a black-and-white photo of a group of people with serious faces wearing old-fashioned clothes. "My middle name is Tzippora, after my grandmother's mother. She's the tall one in the middle of the picture holding the baby. My dad had lots of family in Morocco, a big house with lots of land."

You could see that the kids were impressed by the pictures Shira passed around.

"When my grandfather immigrated to Israel after World War II, he came with most of his extended family. They had to live in tents until they were given a house. What an adjustment! My dad grew up in Jerusalem and met my mom at the university. They got married after he graduated from medical school. I was born a year later! Look, here's a picture of me with my parents and my three little brothers."

"Great job, Shira!" Ariella said. "What a beautiful family! You look just like your mother. Who's next?"

Ariella looked around at the class.

I raised my hand hesitantly.

"Come on up here!" Ariella smiled at me.

My legs were shaking as I walked to the front of the class.

"My name is Meskerem," I said softly, staring at the floor.

Ariella spoke kindly from her desk. "A bit louder, dear."

"My name is Meskerem," I said firmly. "Meskerem is the name of the first month in Amharic."

Silence.

And then the whispers began.

"I knew it. I told you she was Ethiopian!"

"What did I tell you! You see!"

I couldn't continue. My throat choked up, and I felt my eyes beginning to fill with tears.

Luckily, Edna, the principal, chose that exact moment to open the classroom door. She stood in the doorway next to a tall, skinny boy with the largest ears I have ever seen.

"Hello, class. I'd like to introduce you to Robert. He's just moved to Israel from South Africa and will be joining you. Please make him feel welcome. Ariella, can you pair him up with a student who speaks some English to help him get adjusted?"

"Of course," Ariella said and then turned to Robert, speaking very slowly. "Welcome, Robert. Meskerem speaks perfect English, and I'm sure she'd be happy to help you. Please take that seat in the second row next to hers while Meskerem continues her presentation." Turning to Edna, she said, "These are the family tree presentations we discussed. They are fantastic! I am so proud of my students." Ariella beamed.

"Really?" asked Edna. "I'd love to stay and watch."

At least they wouldn't whisper while the principal was in the back of the classroom. I started again.

The urge to cry had passed, but my heart was pounding like a drum, and I just wanted to get it over with.

I unrolled my poster and hung it on the bulletin board. I closed my eyes for a second and touched the Magen David hanging from the chain around my neck. Then I took a deep breath, and suddenly, I heard my voice speak confidently.

"My name is Meskerem. I was born in Israel, in Katzrin. Here is my dad," I continued, pointing at Abba's picture. "He's American Israeli, and he usually

calls me Macy." I looked up, and my eyes met Gadi's. He smiled at me. It was a friendly smile, and I must have looked startled because he looked away quickly toward the window.

The kids were all listening, eyes glued to my poster. "This is my mom. She immigrated to Israel from Ethiopia when she was a bit younger than I am now. My Grandpa Dave lives in America. My Grandma Rose passed away a few years ago. They used to own a hardware store before they retired." I moved my finger to the other side of the family tree. "Here's a picture of my grandma who lives in Katzrin, where I lived before we moved here. The picture of my grandpa is from when he was young. He was killed in the Sudan on the way to Israel."

"Killed! Who killed him?" asked Gadi.

"They were on their way to Sudan on foot when robbers attacked their group." I paused, not sure how much more to say.

"Meskerem, perhaps you could tell us more about Ethiopia?" Ariella suggested, adding, "I understand you made a presentation."

I was surprised that she knew, but I handed her the disk on key with the photos my mom and I had chosen the night before, and she dimmed the lights.

I showed the pictures from Ethiopia, explaining a little about the life in the villages. When I finished, Edna rose and switched on the lights. She gave me a thumbs-up as she slipped out of the room.

Sarah raised her hand.

My stomach tightened.

"Why did you tell us you were from America?" asked Sarah.

Here we go, I thought.

"Uh," I stuttered. "Well. I didn't mean to lie to you." I took a deep breath. For a second the image of the woman taming the lion in Grandma's story flashed before my eyes. I looked straight at the kids in the class and said, "I'm not from America, but I'm not from Ethiopia either. I'm from Israel, but my mom is from Ethiopia. Lots of people think that Ethiopians don't know or understand anything and that they didn't have anything there . . . like, um, clothes and toys and stuff that we have here . . ." My voice faltered.

Ariella joined in. "Many immigrants could not bring their belongings with them to Israel," she explained, "but they brought rich cultural traditions. Being new is never easy, so we must all make an effort to welcome new children to our class, like Meskerem and Robert . . ."

Helen raised her hand. "Do you miss Katzrin?" she asked.

"Do you want us to call you Macy or Meskerem?" Gadi called out.

"I do miss Katzrin, especially my grandma, and the truth is I like my name. Only my dad and my American cousins call me Macy." Suddenly, my voice had become confident, and I said out loud, "Please call me Meskerem."

The bell finally rang, and I walked back to my seat. From the corner of my eye, I saw Sarah pop up and casually drift over to inspect my poster. A couple of other kids crowded around to get a better look at the photos.

"Are those the colors of the Ethiopian flag?" asked Gadi, picking up my pencil case.

"Yes, my grandma embroidered it."

"It's really nice," he admired, running his finger over the letters of my name. "C'mon, let's go catch the picnic table in the yard for lunch!" Gadi started walking toward the classroom door. I stood still, not sure if I'd heard him correctly. He looked back. "You coming?' he asked.

"Sure," I said, and together we headed outside.

About the Author

Naomi Shmuel is the author of more than 15 books, including the first children's books in Hebrew to feature characters of color. Her husband made the long and difficult journey on foot from Ethiopia to Sudan in order to reach Israel, and Naomi began writing for her own children following their encounters with bias. The Hebrew edition of *...too far from home* was an international Hans Christian Andersen Award honor book.

About the Illustrator

Avi Katz, best known as the illustrator of *Jerusalem Report* magazine, has illustrated over 100 books. He lives in Israel.